For Geegee, who is simply the best — A.D.

To my mom and dad, who taught me every day is an opportunity to learn something new — L.A.

About This Book: The illustrations for this book were created using Procreate. This book is set in Tyke Book/ITC. • Text copyright © 2020 by Angela DiTerlizzi • Illustrations copyright © 2020 by Lorena Alvarez • Cover illustration copyright © 2020 by Lorena Alvarez. Cover design by David Hastings. Cover copyright © 2020 by Hachette Book Group, Inc. • Hachette Book Group supports the right to free expression and the value of copyright. The purpose of copyright is to encourage writers and artists to produce the creative works that enrich our culture. • The scanning, uploading, and distribution of this book without permission is a theft of the author's intellectual property. If you would like permission to use material from the book (other than for review purposes), please contact permissions@hbgusa.com. Thank you for your support of the author's rights. • Little, Brown and Company • Hachette Book Group • 1290 Avenue of the Americas, New York, NY 10104 • Visit us at LBYR.com • Originally published in hardcover by Disney • Hyperion, an imprint of Disney Book Group, in April 2020 • First Edition: April 2020 • Little, Brown and Company is a division of Hachette Book Group, Inc. The Little, Brown name and logo are trademarks of Hachette Book Group, Inc. • The publisher is not responsible for websites (or their content) that are not owned by the publisher. • Library of Congress Control Number: 2019945151 • ISBN 978-1-368-02562-1 • PRINTED IN CHINA • APS • 10 9 8 7

THE MAGICAL YET

WORDS BY
Angela DiTerlizzi

ART BY
Lorena Alvarez

L B
LITTLE, BROWN AND COMPANY
New York   Boston

There are days when your dreams haven't come true,
or you're upset by the things you can't do.

If you've lost, or failed, or cried (just a bit),
you're tired of waiting—ready to quit.

Like that shiny, new bike you couldn't ride,
and it didn't matter how hard you tried.

You couldn't pedal and you couldn't steer
and you couldn't get that bike into gear.

Then, when you thought you were on the right track,
you popped a wheelie and fell on your back.

And now you won't ride.
No way. Not never.

No riding for you,
you'll walk . . . forever.

Don't give up now! There's a major game changer—
a most amazing thought rearrange-er!

Someone to show you how good you can get:
Now introducing . . .

The Magical Yet!

With this Yet's magic, you can begin
to see that you're going—beyond where you've been.

There are so many things that you've learned to do
when you didn't know the Yet was with you.

Like when you babbled before you could talk,
or how you crawled before you could walk.

Yet's a dreamer, a schemer,
a hope-er, a try-er—
a maker, a do-er,
a gotta-fly-higher.

This Yet finds a way,
even when you don't.
And Yet knows you will,
when you think you won't.

Like that shiny, new bike
that you couldn't ride—
hop right back on with
the Yet by your side.

Yet doesn't mind warm-ups, fixes, and flops,
do-overs, re-dos, stumbles, and stops.

Yet knows there's mistakes—some big and some small.
With Yet you're sure to get over them all.

Play the kazoo or play the bassoon—
jam with the Yet, and you'll soon be in tune.

Try skateboarding tricks like the Ollie Heelflip. This Yet can get to the championship!

SLOWLY

SNAILS SLID

SLIPPERY

SIX

Tongue twisters twisted
your tongue in a knot?
Yet says, "Keep trying and practice
—*a lot!*"

A BIG

BUG BIT THE

BEETLE

Be patient.

Yet can't do it *all* overnight.

Some things take days, months, or years to get right.

But if you keep leaping,
dreaming, wishing—
waiting, learning,
trying, missing . . .

with the Yet as your guide, along the way,
you'll do all the things you can't do today.

Now you're bolder, braver—starting to see,
with Yet you *can* get where you want to be.

You finally did it! Yet knew you could.
You're not just riding, you're getting quite good!

But don't stop now—you've got so much to do!
The good news is, this Yet grows with you.

So no matter how big (or old) you may get,
you'll never outgrow—you'll never forget—
you can always believe in the magic of Yet.